Emmy
the Exaggerating
Elephant

Fenton
the Fearful Frog

Gertie
the Grungy Goat

He
the Happy
Hamster

the Impatient
Iguana

Ollie
the Obedient
Ostrich

Perry
the Polite
Porcupine

Queenie
the Quiet Quail

Rupert
the Resourceful
Rhinoceros

Wendy
the Wise
Woodchuck

Xavier
the X-ploring
Xenops

Yori
the Yucky Yak

Ziggy
the Zippy Zebra

NOTE TO PARENTS

Emmy, You're the Greatest
A story about moderation

In this story, Emmy the Exaggerating Elephant decides to give a party — the biggest and best party ever. But, true to her character, Emmy buys too much food, too many decorations, and she invites too many guests. There's too much of everything!!! The party becomes a disaster and Emmy is very upset. With the help of her AlphaPet friends, Emmy comes to realize that more is not always better. And even though her party is not the best, the AlphaPets still think Emmy is the greatest because her intentions were good.

In addition to enjoying this humorous story with your child, you can help teach a gentle lesson about the important value of moderation — that too much of a good thing isn't good.

You can also use this story to introduce the letter **E**. As you read about Emmy the Exaggerating Elephant, ask your child to listen for all the **E** words and point to the objects that begin with **E**. When you've finished reading the story, your child will enjoy doing the activity at the end of the book.

The AlphaPets™ characters were conceived and created by Ruth Lerner Perle.
Characters interpreted and designed by Deborah Colvin Borgo.
Cover design by the Antler & Baldwin Design Group.
Book design and production by Publishers' Graphics, Inc.
Logo design by Deborah Colvin Borgo and Nancy S. Norton.

Printed and Manufactured in the United States of America

Emmy,
You're the Greatest

RUTH LERNER PERLE

Illustrated by Deborah Colvin Borgo

Grolier Enterprises Inc.   Danbury, Connecticut

Emmy the Exaggerating Elephant was on her way downtown early one morning when she saw some of her AlphaPet friends.

Toot! Toot! Toot! Emmy honked her horn and waved at them.

"Good Morning, Emmy," said Perry the Polite Porcupine, tipping his cap. "Nice day!"

"Nice day!" exclaimed Emmy. "It's not just a *nice* day! It's a gorgeous, glorious, *magnificent* day. The sky's the bluest, the sun's the brightest, and the grass is the greenest it's ever been."

"Well, aren't *you* the cheery one!" said Una the Unhappy Unicorn. "Why get all excited? It's a day like every other day. Nothing to do. Nowhere to go. Boring, boring, boring."

"Mmm," added Queenie the Quiet Quail.

"Where's your enthusiasm?" cried Emmy. "It's the *most* beautiful day I've ever seen! A great day for a celebration — for a party! That's it! I'll throw a party! It will be the biggest and best party in the whole wide world. "Hop in!" she shouted. "Hold on to your hats, and away we go!"

The AlphaPets piled into Emmy's car and rode off in a cloud of dust.

Emmy's car screeched to a stop in front of the Eleven Elves Shopping Emporium. "Follow me!" she said, and they all ran toward the entrance of the shopping center.

On the way, Emmy invited everyone she saw to come to her party. "Good morning, shoppers," she called. "Come to my party! It will be the absolute greatest! Bring all your friends!"

Emmy stepped on the escalator. "Hey, everybody!" she shouted. "You're *all* invited to a big bash at my place."

Yori the Yucky Yak said, "I think parties are yucky. Too much laughing and singing and dancing. My spiders get nervous at parties. And so do I."

"I never know what to say at parties," said Fenton.

"I never know what to say at parties, either," agreed Monty the Mimicking Mouse.

"Don't worry about a thing," whooped Emmy. "Everyone will love *this* party, even your spiders, Yori. And there will be a special super-duper surprise at the end. You won't want to miss that!"

"Wow! Everyone in town wants to come to my party!" cried Emmy. "How exciting! I must be sure to have more than enough of everything and I *must* have an extra, extra special surprise."

Everyone followed Emmy to the food store, where she bought:

dozens of eggs,

gallons of milk,

crates of crackers,

sacks of sandwiches,

wheels of cheese,

buckets of biscuits,

gobs of gumdrops,

jugs of jellybeans,

rafts of raisins, berries, and nuts.

Then she bought:

tubs of ice cream,

piles of pizza,

and pounds of popcorn, pretzels, and chips.

The shopping carts were so full that the checkout clerk couldn't see who was doing the shopping.

"You won't be able to carry all this," said the clerk. "You're buying too much."

"Never mind," said Emmy from behind her bundles. "My friends will help me. Please leave the packages at the pick-up counter and we'll get them on the way out."

Next, everyone followed Emmy to the party goods store. Emmy ordered hundreds of balloons in every size and color, giant bags of confetti, cases of crepe paper streamers, and yards of electric lights and lanterns.

She also bought piles of paper plates, heaps of hats, horns and noisemakers, and boxes full of cups, forks, spoons, and straws.

And along the way, she kept inviting more and more guests.

After the AlphaPets
finished shopping,
they squeezed into
the elevator and
rode down.

They picked up the
groceries and loaded
all the bags and
boxes into Emmy's car.

"And now," said Emmy, with a twinkle in her eye, "I'm off! But no one can go with me now. This part is a secret.

"Go home, everybody, and come to my house tonight at exactly eight o'clock. Be sure to wear your most elegant party clothes."

"Excuse me, but will we all fit into your house?" asked Perry.

"Oh, dear, I didn't think about that," said Emmy. But then she smiled and said, "We'll have the party outside!"

Emmy jumped into her car. She buckled her seatbelt, and *vroom*!, off she went.

As she swerved around the corner, Emmy heard a rattle and a crash! Packages and bags and boxes were falling helter-skelter, everywhere. Eggs cracked, balloons popped, and games rolled all over the street.

"Oh, dear," said Emmy, watching the balloons escape. "I hope I still have enough of everything." And she ran into the bakery after cleaning up the mess.

Meanwhile, all the AlphaPets were getting ready for the party. As soon as the town clock struck eight, they came rushing from every direction.

When the AlphaPets arrived at the party, they could hardly believe their eyes and ears.

EVERYBODY WELCOME to EMMY'S EXTRAVAGANZA!

Music was blaring from eleven loudspeakers. There were hundreds of balloons and decorations and thousands of electric lights. And giant tables were loaded with mountains of food.

But the party was much too noisy . . .

Perry tried to greet his friends but nobody could hear him.

It was too bright . . .

"I can't see anything," complained Una. "Those bright lights are blinding me."

It was too crowded . . .

There were so many people that Yori was afraid his spiders would be crushed.

And, it was too messy . . .

The ice cream was melting.

The fudge was dripping.

The soda fountain was overflowing.

The pizzas were falling.

And popcorn was popping everywhere!

ZZZZAP!!! CRACKLE!!!

Suddenly, the music stopped and all of the lights went out.

"Oh no! Help! Help!" shouted Fenton.

"Help! Help!" shouted Monty.

Bradley the Brave Bear turned on his flashlight.

"I guess the power blew," he said. "We used too much electricity."

"Emmy had better call for help," said Delilah the Demanding Duck. "Where is Emmy anyway? And where's the big surprise she promised us?"

Just then, a giant van arrived. The back door opened, and down the ramp rolled the biggest, pinkest, gooiest cake the AlphaPets had ever seen.

"So *this* is the surprise!" cried Perry.

"But where is Emmy?" asked Fenton. "Is she hurt? Or sick? Or lost?"

Suddenly, the frosting on top of the cake started to wiggle. The sprinkles started to wriggle, and the jelly started to jiggle.

SPLAT!

The cake split open and *out* leaped Emmy with a great, big smile on her face.

Emmy looked around and saw what happened to the food and decorations.

"Oh, dear," she cried. "I wanted this party to be the best and greatest party that ever was. But I did too much. Everything is ruined."

"More is not always better," said Wendy the Wise Woodchuck.

"That's true," Perry agreed. "Maybe the party wasn't so great, but *you* are, Emmy. You tried your very best to give us all a good time."

Enjoy these exciting words with me!

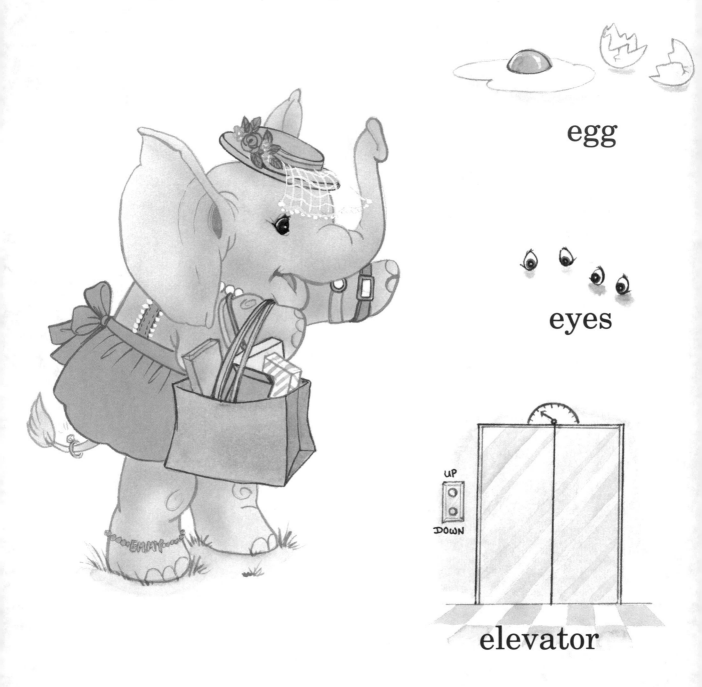

egg

eyes

elevator

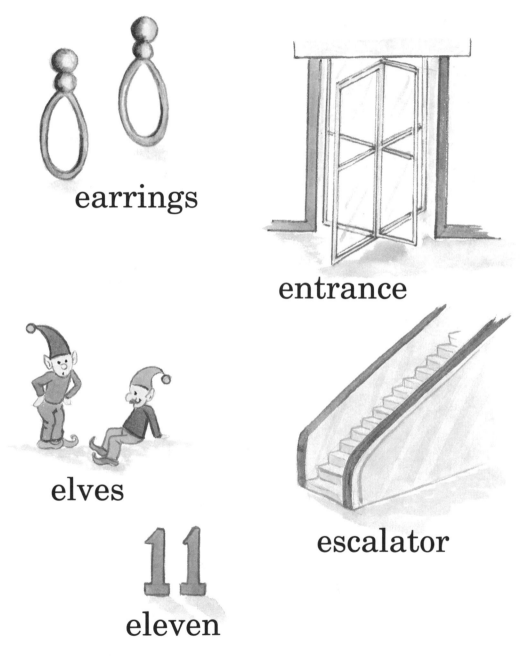

earrings

entrance

elves

11

eleven

escalator

Look back at the pictures in this book and try to find these and other things that begin with the letter E.

Know Your Alphabet

Aa Bb

Gg Hh

Mm Nn Oo Pp

Uu Vv Ww